Live! In Concert!

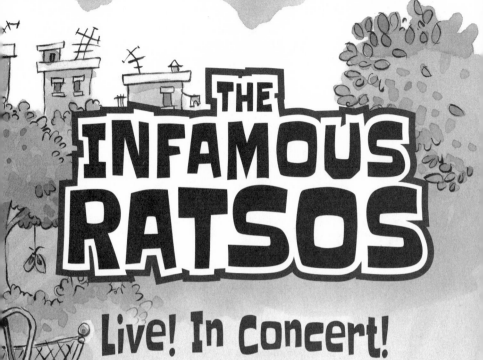

THE INFAMOUS RATSOS

Live! In Concert!

Kara LaReau

illustrated by Matt Myers

CANDLEWICK PRESS

Text copyright © 2022 by Kara LaReau
Illustrations copyright © 2022 by Matt Myers

First edition 2022

Library of Congress Catalog Card Number 2021947421
ISBN 978-1-5362-0747-7

22 23 24 25 26 27 LBM 10 9 8 7 6 5 4 3 2 1

Printed in Melrose Park, IL, USA

This book was typeset in Scala.
The illustrations were done in ink and watercolor dye on paper.

Candlewick Press
99 Dover Street
Somerville, Massachusetts 02144

www.candlewick.com

For Sarah, who trusts that my ideas
will work out in the end
KL

For Hayley, best rat wrangler in the Big City
or anyplace else
MM

REAL CHANGES

I love a good picnic in the park," Big Lou says. "I'm just not sure about this background music."

"*We're the Critter Kidz*
and we're here to say
love yourselves, love each other
each and every day . . ."

Tiny sings as he and Millicent and Velma have fun dancing on the old bandstand stage.

"This song is by the Critter Kidz," Ralphie says, snapping his fingers. "How can you not like their music?"

"I guess it really isn't meant for an old critter like me," Big Lou says.

"It's meant for everyone," Ralphie says.

"You have to admit, Tiny's got moves," Louie says. "And Millicent and Velma aren't too bad, either."

"In every way, let your true self show. Don't be afraid—let the whole world know," Tiny continues.

"Let your true self show!" sings Millicent.

"Let the whole world know!" sings Velma.

"They sound pretty good, too," says Ralphie. "Almost as good as the real thing."

"They'd sound better if the bandstand still had a working sound system," Big Lou says. He looks around. "When I was your age, this park was in great shape. It's really gone downhill over the years."

"Mama was working to fix things at the park, wasn't she?" Louie asks. Mama Ratso died a little while ago, but as long as Louie and Ralphie and Big Lou remember her, they're not so sad.

"She was on the Neighborhood Parks Committee," Big Lou says. "She had ideas for some real changes around here. Too bad she wasn't able to make them happen. Since she's been gone, things have *really* fallen apart."

"We can't even play on the playground anymore, since most of the equipment is rusted or broken," Ralphie says.

"Listen up, all you boys and girls," sings Millicent.

"Let's come together and change the world!" sings Velma.

"I think I'm going to go up there and join them," Ralphie says. "I really love this song."

"This park reminds me so much of your mother," Big Lou says, smiling. "If she was still around, she'd know how to get things done around here."

Louie is listening, but he's also watching Ralphie and Tiny and Millicent and Velma sing and dance.

"Listen up," sings Tiny.

"Boys and girls," sings Millicent.

"Come together," sings Velma.

"You can change the WORLD!" sings Ralphie.

And that's when Louie gets an idea.

"I think I might know how to get a few things done around here, too," he says.

2

WAIT FOR IT

You guys look like you're having a lot of fun," Louie says to Tiny and Millicent and Velma and Ralphie.

"I was born to be onstage," Tiny says.

"He's not wrong," says Millicent.

"I just love the Critter Kidz," says Velma.

"Me, too," says Ralphie. "Their songs make me feel good."

"Well, I know another way you could feel good," Louie says. "I have an idea."

"Uh-oh," says Velma. "I've heard about your ideas."

"It's true. Not all of my brother's ideas are great—" Ralphie admits.

"Hey!" says Louie.

"But they always work out in the end," Ralphie adds.

"This idea has to do with singing and dancing," Louie says.

"I'm listening," says Tiny.

"I want to organize a fundraising concert to pay for new playground equipment at the Big City Park and maybe even a new sound system for the bandstand. We'll have the concert right here. You four can perform some Critter Kidz songs."

"Wouldn't we get into trouble singing Critter Kidz songs?" Velma asks.

"Leave all that to me," Louie says.

"Would people really come to watch us perform?" Ralphie asks.

"If you keep singing and dancing like that, they will," Louie says.

"Ooh! I can make some really cool sets," says Millicent. "And Fluffy knows how to sew. We can ask her if she'll make costumes for us!"

"Hold on a minute," Tiny says.

"What?" Louie asks. "You don't think it's a good idea?"

"No—I just thought of the name of our group," Tiny says. He strikes a dramatic pose. "Wait for it."

"We're waiting," says Ralphie.

Tiny throws open his arms. "THE BIG CITY CRITTER KIDZ!" he cries.

"It really is perfect," says Millicent.

"I know," says Tiny.

"It's a good thing you're talented *and* humble," says Louie.

3

SO . . . GIRLY

I've talked to the Critter Kidz' people," Louie informs everyone at lunch that week. "It turns out they love working with kids raising money for good causes. So we can use their songs if we sell their merchandise at the concert—they'll even donate part of the proceeds to our fundraising effort."

"I can't believe all of you are going to sing and dance onstage, in front of everyone," Chad says. "You couldn't *pay* me to get up there."

"It's OK, Chad. Not everyone has what it takes to be a star," Tiny says. "I've been practicing my singing and working on our choreography every chance I get."

"And I've been working on your costumes," Fluffy says. She shows everyone her notebook. "Here are my latest sketches."

"Oooh!" says Millicent. "I LOVE all the glitter and sequins!"

"More for me, please," Tiny says.

"Glitter? And sequins?" Chad laughs. "Those look so . . . girly."

"I based these on the real Critter Kidz' costumes," Fluffy explains.

"Well, they're fine for Millicent and Velma," Chad says. "But for Tiny and Ralphie, you two are going to look like GIRLS up there."

"The real Critter Kidz are Ronnie, Bobbi, Ricki, and Mike," Velma informs Chad. "Ronnie and Mike are boys, and *they* wear glitter and sequins."

"And anyway, who cares? I'm going to look like *myself* up there," Tiny says. "Right, Ralphie?"

"Uh . . . right," Ralphie says. But the more he looks at Fluffy's sketches and thinks about Chad's words, the more he's not so sure.

- 4 -

NO TALKING
AND NO
SINGING

More meatloaf, please," Louie says, holding out his plate.

"That's your third helping," Big Lou says, piling it on.

"And more mashed potatoes, too," Louie says. "I need all the energy

I can get. I have a LOT to do before the concert."

"Ralphie, you've barely touched your food. Don't you need your energy, too? You're the one who's going to be performing, after all," Big Lou says.

Ralphie sighs. "I don't feel like eating. OR performing."

"What?" Louie says.

"I thought you loved the Critter Kidz," Big Lou says.

"I do," says Ralphie. "I just don't know if I want to get up there in front of everyone to sing and dance and . . . wear that costume."

"Are you worried about what Chad said?" Louie asks.

"What did Chad say?" Big Lou says.

"That Tiny and I are going to look like GIRLS up there," Ralphie says. "Everyone's going to laugh at us."

Big Lou puts down his fork.

"Anyone who thinks looking or acting like a girl is something to be ashamed of has another thing coming," Big Lou says. "Your mama was a girl. Grandma Ratso is a girl. Some of the strongest, smartest, bravest people I've known have been girls."

"Me, too. Like Millicent, and Velma, and Fluffy," says Louie.

"And my teacher, Miss Beavers," Ralphie adds. "So then why is 'girly' supposed to be a bad thing?"

"Some people think being male means being the opposite of female, so it means we're supposed to act a certain way, or only like certain things. Like we're all in boxes, with limits on who we can be," Big Lou says. "If that was true, I wouldn't be able to do the things I really love, like birdwatching and cooking and baking."

"The things we like should have nothing to do with whether we're boys or girls," says Louie.

"I don't want to be in a box," Ralphie says. "That seems . . . uncomfortable."

"It's uncomfortable, unhealthy, and definitely *no fun*," Big Lou says. "Try focusing on how you feel and not on what other people think."

"OK, I'll try," says Ralphie. "But first I'd like to try another helping of mashed potatoes."

Big Lou is just about to give Ralphie an extra dollop when the apartment buzzer goes off.

"Hello?" Louie asks. But no one answers.

"Who is it?" Big Lou asks.

"I don't know. I'm going to go downstairs to find out," Louie says.

"Wait for me," says Ralphie. "I love a mystery."

Louie opens the door. "Tiny?"

But Tiny doesn't say anything. He takes off his backpack and rifles around in it. He takes out a notebook and a pencil.

"What's wrong?" Ralphie asks.

I have laryngitis, Tiny writes.

"Laryngitis?" Louie says.

I think I practiced too much, Tiny writes. Now when I sing, nothing comes out. The doctor says no talking and no singing for a <u>whole week.</u>

"Uh-oh," Ralphie says. "I don't think we can go on without Tiny. He's the best singer and dancer!"

Louie grabs Ralphie by the shoulders. "Don't flake on me now, brother. I need you. The park needs you!"

The Big City Critter Kidz need you, writes Tiny.

"I promise we'll find someone to take Tiny's place tomorrow," Louie says.

Good luck, Tiny writes. You have big shoes to fill.

- 5 -

THE SHOW MUST GO ON

OK, who's our next audition?" Velma asks.

Louie consults his clipboard. "You mean who's our *last* audition," he says.

Tiny shows them his notebook. This better be good, it says.

"I'm with Tiny," Millicent says, sighing. "I don't know if I can take much more of this."

"Hey, everyone," Sid Chitterer announces. "I heard you were looking for a star performer."

"I didn't know Sid sang," Velma says to Louie.

Sid puts his hand under his shirt. He proceeds to make armpit farts to the tune of "Twinkle, Twinkle, Little Star."

BLAPPLE, BLAPPLE, BLAPPLE BLAP!

Louie sighs.

"He can't," he mutters.

"Wanna hear my encore?" Sid offers. "I can burp the whole alphabet!"

Tiny claps and shows Sid his notebook.

Thank you, it says. Our people will call your people.

"We've held auditions for three days, and we've seen and heard everyone on the list," Louie says, examining his clipboard. "No one even comes *close*."

"And my ears hurt," Millicent says.

I told you it would be hard to replace me, Tiny writes in his notebook.

"Hey, everyone, I just finished all the costumes!" Fluffy says. "Intro-ducing… one of the soon-to-be-world-famous Big City Critter Kidz!"

Ralphie takes the stage.

"Whoa," Louie says.

"You look *amazing*, Ralphie!" Millicent says.

"You did a great job, Fluffy," Ralphie says. "It makes me feel like a real Critter Kid!"

"Well, if it isn't Ralphiella Ratso," Chad says.

"Quit it, Chad," Louie says.

"What are you even doing here?" Velma asks.

"I heard Louie was looking for microphones and speakers," Chad says.

"I am," Louie says. "Do you know someone?"

"Yeah. Me," Chad replies. "You can pick them up from my place, if you want. That is, when Ralphie's done with his *fashion show*."

"Aw, come on," Ralphie says.

"Didn't you get the memo, Ratso? Or maybe you *like* all that corny singing and dancing and those sparkly costumes?" Chad says. "Everyone knows the Critter Kidz are for *girls*."

"Liking the Critter Kidz is for boys *and* girls," Ralphie insists.

"And what's your problem with girls, Chad?" Millicent asks. "You *wish* you could be as cool as me."

"Or as smart as me," says Velma.

"Or as talented as me," says Fluffy.

"Whatever," Chad says. "Have fun, *ladies.*"

"Wow. What's up with him?" asks Velma.

Chad gets cranky when he's hungry, Tiny writes.

"Well, he must be *starving*," Velma says.

"I should probably go to Chad's apartment now so I have time to set everything up at the bandstand," Louie says.

"You're going to accept help from him?" Millicent asks Louie. "After the way he's been acting?"

"Where else am I going to get the equipment for the concert?" Louie says, shrugging.

"Chad's right, anyway," Ralphie says, taking off his costume. "I can't wear this. And I can't be in the show, especially if I'm the only boy. It's all too . . ."

"What? 'Girly?'" Millicent says. "I'd expect that from Chad, but not you, Ralphie."

"Remember what Dad said: focus on how you feel, not on what other people think," Louie reminds him.

Ralphie closes his eyes. He imagines everyone laughing at him onstage and he feels . . . pretty awful.

"Well, I don't care what Chad thinks. My costumes look great," Fluffy says.

Do I still get one? Tiny asks.

"Of course," Fluffy says. "I'd never leave you out."

"But with Tiny *and* Ralphie out of the show, we're down *two* Big City Critter Kidz," Velma reminds everyone. "What now?"

"I wish I could do it. But I can't sing or dance," says Fluffy.

"Me, neither," Louie says. "But the show must go on."

"How?" Millicent asks.

"I'll think of something," Louie says. "Like my brother says, my ideas always work out in the end."

6

A LITTLE TWIST

I've never been to Chad's apartment before," Louie says as the Ratso brothers walk through the Big City. "Have you?"

Ralphie shakes his head. He doesn't feel like talking. He can't stop thinking about Big Lou's words: "Try focusing on how you feel and not on what other people think."

Ever since he walked off the bandstand stage, Ralphie's been feeling a little twist in his stomach.

"This is it." Louie double-checks his clipboard, then hits the apartment buzzer. "We won't stay too long. I just need to get the equipment, and then we'll go."

"Hello?" a lady's voice on the intercom says.

"It's Louie and Ralphie Ratso," Louie says. "We're here to see Chad."

BZZZZZT goes the door, letting Louie and Ralphie in.

"We're in the middle of rewatching last night's game," Mr. Badgerton informs them. "We don't like to be interrupted."

"Nonsense, Thad. I've made plenty of snacks for everyone. It's nice to finally meet you Ratso boys," says Mrs. Badgerton. "Chad talks about you all the time."

"Not *all* the time," Chad says.

Chad's older brother Brad laughs. "You two are the ones organizing that corny concert in the park," he says.

"It's not corny. It's for *charity*," Louie explains.

"I heard you're going to be singing and dancing like the Critter Kidz,"

Brad says. "Did you know Chad used to *love* the Critter Kidz?"

"Shut up, Brad," Chad says.

"It's true," Brad says. "He'd sing *all* their songs. And he did all their corny moves."

"When I was a *baby*. Because the Critter Kidz are for babies. And girls," Chad says, rolling his eyes. "You'd never catch me singing their songs now."

"Me, neither," Ralphie says, nodding. But when he says it, he feels that little twist again.

"Any chance we could get back to watching this *game*?" Mr. Badgerton asks.

"Come on," Chad says to Louie and Ralphie. "The equipment's in my room."

"Have fun with your *girlfriends*, Chad," Brad says.

"We're not his—" Ralphie starts to explain.

Louie pulls him toward Chad's room. "Don't bother," he says. "It's pretty clear he's not worth it."

"Let me know if you boys want snacks!" Mrs. Badgerton yells after them.

"Wow," Louie says, looking around Chad's room. "You really love cars and planes and sports."

"And books and movies . . . about cars and planes and sports," Ralphie notes.

"I guess I just like cool stuff. Like my dad and my brother," Chad says.

"I like movies, too," Ralphie says. "My favorite is *The Mousetrap Mystery*."

"Never heard of it. Does it have cars or planes or sports in it?" Chad says.

"No," Ralphie says.

"Well, that's probably why," says Chad. "Hey, are you OK, Ralphie?"

"It's just . . . a little stomachache," Ralphie says.

"I bet you're hungry. I know I'm hungry," says Chad. "I'll go get us some of those snacks my mom made."

"What's wrong with you?" Louie asks Ralphie after Chad leaves.

"Nothing," he says. "I'm fine."

And that's when Ralphie's stomach starts to feel *really* twisty.

"Ouch!" he says, doubling over. He loses his balance and falls right into Chad's shelf. A big box topples to the floor.

"Ralphie, are you OK?" Louie asks. But Ralphie isn't paying attention to Louie, or to his stomach. He's staring at the contents of the box.

"Wait. Is that what I think it is?" Louie asks. He leans in to get a closer look.

Inside the box, the Ratso brothers see . . . Critter Kidz posters.

And magazines.

And stickers.

And dolls.

And a Critter Kidz costume, just like the ones Fluffy made.

"It's . . . a Critter Kidz shrine," Ralphie whispers.

"Hidden in a *box*. Just like Dad said," says Louie.

CRASH!

7

CROSS OUR HEARTS

We're sorry, Chad," Louie says.

"We didn't snoop on purpose," Ralphie tries to explain. "I tripped, and the box fell off the shelf."

"This is . . . my old stuff. From when I was a baby," Chad says. "I've been meaning to throw it out for a while."

"But isn't that poster from the Critter Kidz' latest tour?" Ralphie says. "And I just bought those stickers a few weeks ago from Clawmart."

"And that costume looks like it would fit you now," Louie notes.

Chad slides to the floor. "Please don't tell anyone. Especially my dad and my brother." And then he starts to cry.

Ralphie looks at Louie. Louie looks at Ralphie. They have never, ever seen Chad cry before.

The Ratso brothers close Chad's bedroom door. They sit on the floor with him.

"We promise we won't tell anyone," Ralphie says.

"Cross our hearts," says Louie. "But why does it have to be such a secret?"

"My brother started making fun of me for liking the Critter Kidz a while ago. He says it's corny and silly and girly. Now I just do stuff with him and my dad," Chad explains. "I thought about throwing all my stuff away, but I just couldn't do it. It almost made me sick."

"I know how that feels," Ralphie says, holding his stomach.

"So I put it all in this box, and I take everything out and sing and dance in secret," Chad says.

"Do you even *like* cars and planes and sports?" Louie asks.

"They're OK," Chad says. "Mostly I like them because Brad and my dad like them."

"It doesn't seem fun to only like the things other people like. And to have to hide your favorite stuff in a box," Louie says.

"My dad says we should care about how we feel, not what other people think," Ralphie says. "At first, I felt awful, imagining that people were going to laugh at me onstage at the concert. But I feel worse for quitting, when singing and dancing to the Critter Kidz makes me so happy."

"The Critter Kidz make me happy, too," says Chad. "Wow, that feels really good to say."

"It does," says Ralphie. For the first time all afternoon, his stomach doesn't hurt at all.

"So . . . that costume really fits you?" Louie asks Chad. "And you know all the songs and moves?"

"Sure," says Chad. "Why?"

Ralphie looks at his brother.

"I know that look," he says to Louie. "You have an idea."

"Yep. Probably the biggest one yet," Louie says. He reaches for his clipboard.

"I think we're going to need more snacks," says Chad.

8

BREAK A LEG

I'm nervous," Millicent says, peeking through the gap in the curtain.

"Wow," says Velma. "Everyone in the neighborhood is here."

"I see my dad!" says Ralphie. "He's sitting next to Mr. Nutzel and Mrs. Porcupini . . . and my grandma and grandpa!"

"All the kids from school are here, too," Louie says. "And all the teachers, and Principal Otteriguez."

"I see my mom. With my dad . . . and Brad," says Chad.

"Stop fidgeting. I need to fix this row of sequins," Fluffy says.

"I can't help it. I'm nervous," says Chad. "I know all the songs and all the steps, but it's been a long time since I've sung and danced in front of people. Especially my dad . . . and Brad. What if they laugh, or worse?"

Ralphie puts his hand on Chad's shoulder. "We're all in this together," he says. "Just remember: focus on how you feel and not on what other people think."

"OK," Chad says. "I'll try."

"I'm going out there," Louie says. "Break a leg, everyone!"

"Ugh, now I have to be worried about *breaking a leg*, too?" Chad moans.

"It's just a saying," Velma says. "In show business, it means good luck!"

"Ladies and gentlemen!" Louie shouts. "Thanks to everyone for coming out tonight and supporting the Big City Park. My mom always said that if you want the world to be a better place, you should start in your own backyard. Well, for a lot of us, this park is our backyard. So we're here to do what we can to make some real changes. Without further ado, put your hands together for . . . *The Big City Critter Kidz!*"

Everyone in the audience claps. Except for Brad. His arms are crossed, and he's smirking.

Tiny turns on the spotlight. Louie turns on the music.

Then the curtain opens.

"We're the Critter Kidz and we're here to say," sings Millicent.

"Love yourselves, love each other each and every day," sings Velma.

"In every way, let your true self show. Don't be afraid—let the whole world know," sings Ralphie.

"Let your true self show!" sings Millicent.

"Let the whole world know!" sings Velma.

"Listen up, all you boys and girls. Let's come together and change the world!" sings Chad.

"Listen up," sings Velma.

"All you boys and girls," sings Millicent.

"Come together," sings Ralphie.

"And change the world," sings Chad.

"AND! CHANGE! THE! WORLD!" they all sing together.

After that song, they sing another, and another, and another. When the Big City Critter Kidz finish, the audience goes wild. Big Lou is the first to give them a standing ovation, then everyone else gets to their feet, too. Including Chad's dad.

"That's my boy up there," Mr. Badgerton says, hugging Chad's

mom. "Where's he been hiding all that talent?"

"Bradley, stand up and clap for your brother," Mrs. Badgerton says.

"No way," Brad says. "It's corny. And silly. And *girly*."

"Stand up, son," says Mr. Badgerton. "Your brother's a *star*!"

"Whatever," Brad says, standing up. "I could sing and dance better than him, if I wanted to."

As Millicent and Velma and Ralphie and Chad take their bows, Grandma

Ratso puts her fingers in her mouth and whistles.

"We want to thank Fluffy Rabbitski for the costumes, Millicent Stanko for the scenery, Tiny Crawley for the choreography, and the original Critter Kidz for the music," Louie announces.

Fluffy and Tiny come onstage and take a bow with Millicent.

"And we want to thank Louie for organizing this whole thing," Ralphie says. "We couldn't have done this without my big brother."

"We raised a lot of money tonight," Louie says, looking at his clipboard. "Maybe not enough to pay for new playground equipment and a sound system for the bandstand, but it's a good start."

As everyone gives another round of applause and Louie takes his bow, a big black car pulls up right outside the park gates.

"Who's that?" Louie asks.

"Ooh, maybe it's the real Critter Kidz!" Ralphie says.

"Ronnie, Bobbi, Ricki, and Mike are *here?*" Millicent asks.

"It can't be. They're on tour until the end of next month," Chad informs her.

"You're right. It's not them," Big Lou says, squinting at the license plate. "It's *another* Big City celebrity."

9

PLACES, EVERYONE!

Mayor Fluffman?" Louie says as the Big City mayor emerges from his limousine and makes his way up to the bandstand stage.

"Ladies and gentlemen!" Mayor Fluffman greets everyone. "As soon as I heard about this worthy event, I knew I had to show my support. This park is the heart of our fair city, and I was so moved to hear that some of our fine youths have taken matters into their own hands to improve their neighborhood."

"It was our mama's idea first," Ralphie explains.

"She was on the Neighborhood Parks Committee," Louie adds. "When she was alive, she wanted the best for us—for all of us."

"I remember your mother and how much she wanted to make things better around here," Mayor Fluffman says. "So the city will add to whatever you've raised tonight, to make sure you have enough to improve the playground *and* the bandstand."

Everyone in the crowd claps. Grandma Ratso lets loose with one of her signature whistles.

"And . . . we'll be christening the playground with this special plaque," the mayor adds. One of his aides unveils it for the audience.

"'The Rita Ratso Memorial Playground,'" Louie reads.

"You're naming it . . . after Mama?" Ralphie says.

Mayor Fluffman nods. "She was all about making changes around here," he says. "This change feels right."

"I'm so proud of you boys. Your mother would be, too," Big Lou says, wiping away a tear.

"Woo-hoo! This calls for a celebration!" Grandpa Ratso yells.

"Even better," says Louie. "This calls for an *encore*."

Places, everyone! Tiny announces.

"Whew! Are we really going to do *more?*" Chad asks.

"You know what they say," Ralphie says. "The show must go on!"